CAUGHT LOOKING BY THE JOCK

Straight to Gay First Time Story

Michael Levi

ISBN: 9798421855170
Imprint: Independently published

1st edition

Cover design by: Michael Levi

CONTENTS

CHAPTER 1

He stepped into the room and I couldn't look away. Really, I didn't know what was going on with me and, to make matters worse, he closed the door. I felt like I was all alone with the guy, which couldn't be the truth.

I was just putting on my shirt and I felt incredibly uncomfortable that we were in the same place, sharing the same room, and I couldn't stop looking at him.

Then, he turned his eyes slightly in my direction. He gave me a glance and then resumed what he was doing. He went to his locker, popped open the door, and then fished out a white towel. He rubbed it at his face, looking a little less sweaty now.

The sun was quite intense and bright outside, making any game of soccer feel so strenuous and tiresome. I didn't know how my friend could play there outside for so long without passing out. Really, he appeared to be some kind of stamina freak, though I didn't like thinking about him that way.

Ed was just unlike anyone I knew and the role model I never thought I'd find. I wished I could become more like him one day. I was pretty sure it would never happen, but the possibility was in the air.

He tossed the towel into a bin even though he didn't need to. I was kind of paralyzed where I was. My eyes diverting to the bin, I couldn't help but feel like going there and taking a sniff of it. It was just so unfortunate that it would never happen, though.

One of the reasons why I felt uncomfortable in his presence was his perfect body. And when I said perfect, I really meant it.

I couldn't help but wonder what my dating life would be like if I had a similar body. I calmed myself down by hammering into my mind that it would never happen, no matter how hard I tried.

That didn't mean I was gay or anything like that, though. I mean, really, the thought of that being the case was ridiculous. I never thought about a man that way, even though there had been times when I thought it would happen.

Ed looked at me again, opening a faint smile. It was a little weak, but it was also showing off his confidence. I remembered that he was a little taller than me, which immediately put me in a very submissive position. Even though I knew I should hate it, I kept falling into it and I knew Ed was using that to his advantage.

I took a deep breath in, Ed holding out his hand. It was so big and heavy. That was just how it was. Ed wasn't just bigger than me, but his hand also made me feel so tiny and like nothing before him.

I took his hand and felt how firm his handshake was. He pulled me to him and we bumped shoulders, my bare skin touching his for the first time today. I didn't know what was about him, but Ed always liked touching people, even when he didn't need to. He just liked doing that, which didn't help with reminding me that I was straight and would never experiment.

His skin was as if it was shining under the lights of the room, looking very smooth and soft. Once again, I wanted to touch it more intimately, but I reminded myself that it would never happen.

"How are you doing, man? You look... a little off," he commented, making me snap right back to reality. The last thing I needed was Ed finding out that I thought of him as my role model.

He wasn't the kind of guy that held back when it came to bullying people online, and I didn't want to become his next prey. I could still remember what he and his other mates did when they found out that a fellow student was gay.

They bullied him so much that he ended up moving to another college, which was brutal and a good reminder that, in here, everyone was like that. Religion and toxicity were everywhere in this place.

"Sorry, it's nothing. You just caught me thinking about my finals. Studying is killing me, man."

"Maybe you should think about doing something different," he proposed, retreating his hand and making me miss it, even though it didn't make any sense. I didn't know what was going on with me right now, but it was as though seeing this dominating and imposing man about my age was sprouting something in me I thought I didn't have.

"Like what?" I asked, wondering if he was even going to propose a worthwhile solution or was just going to crack a joke about it.

"How about putting more effort into becoming a proper soccer player, like me?" He asked, looking directly into my eyes and making me wonder if something else was going on in his mind.

The ring on his finger didn't lie about his engagement status right now. He had a girlfriend – a pretty one – and even though I'd thought of her a couple of times when I was jacking off, it always happened when Ed was involved, too. It was yet one more thing about me he should never know about.

"I'm not so sure about that," I confessed, feeling yet even more uncomfortable. Compared to him, my body was quite lean and it lacked the definition he had.

He turned toward the locker, grabbed his clothes, and I turned to my locker. I was in the locker room before he showed up because I got injured and told the mister that I couldn't keep going.

"See, sometimes that's your problem. You don't know what you're doing with your life, and let me tell you, that's a little annoying," he pointed out, going to the bathroom.

Goodness me. I didn't remember, until now, that he took

showers every time after he played. He went there and I followed him from behind. It was one of those open-space bathrooms, and I didn't even know what I was thinking I was doing by going there. Was I thinking that we were going to talk a little more and get to know each other better? I didn't know but, at this point, I couldn't contain my desire to go there with him. I just had to go.

It wasn't the first time that we were going to shower together, but this time things were different. My mind wanted to find something that I shouldn't look at.

He opened the door, lowered his shorts, tossed them into a bin for used uniform pieces, and then I followed him. I took off my clothes too, got under one of the showerheads, and tried not to say anything.

I was with my back turned to him, just in case he noticed my erection. It wasn't that I was finding this hot or anything like that, but that it was stirring something in me I hadn't felt in a very long time.

I was attracted to girls, but this was something different. I was showering together with my mate.

I couldn't stop thinking about what his body looked like now that he didn't have his clothes on.

Not giving that much thought, the first thing I did was peer over my shoulder. Ed was happily soaping up his body, moving his hands over his abs. The light and the water made them look even more defined, shadows dancing where they were.

Just like all the other times, I couldn't help but wonder what it would be like to have a similar body. I was pretty sure that my life would be just like his. Pretty much everyone in college would be falling on their knees for me.

And just as I was doing that, he suddenly lifted his head and I had to turn mine away. Not wishing to show him that I was doing something wrong, my heart was a little tight as I thought he was going to realize I was looking.

It didn't look like Ed was going to say anything, though he was whistling gently while he kept soaping up his body and washing it. I could hear his fingers rubbing against something, and I knew that it was his hair. He was almost finished with his shower, as was I.

"Tell me, Andrew, would you be interested in coming home with me right now?"

"Right now?" I asked, almost wishing he hadn't said that. I knew I couldn't say no. It was difficult saying 'no' to someone that was pretty much my role model and I had a submissive relationship with.

"That's right. I'm going to have dinner there with some of my friends, and I'd like to have you there with us."

CHAPTER 2

I didn't know what was going on in his mind, but it had been difficult saying no. Ed had such a hold on me it was complicated putting it into words. I was looking at him over my shoulder and I couldn't stop admiring his perfect body. There was just something about it that kept drawing me to it.

"Cat got your tongue?" He asked, smiling devilishly. He knew the weight of his request and that it was difficult for me to say no. Not thinking too much about that, I knew I had just one answer I could give him.

"Sure, man. Why not?" I said, hoping that I was making the right choice and that I wasn't going to do anything I would regret later.

He turned off the showerhead, turning around so that I could see his butt. If I thought that his cock was perfect, I was now even more impressed. His asscheeks were lust-inducing, making me want to touch them even though I knew that was very gay and I shouldn't be thinking that way regarding my mate.

It was as though time was passing much more slowly as he grabbed one of the towels and started to dry his body with it. I didn't know what was going on with me, but I could still feel the water running down my body and I knew that I was still where I was, right in the bathroom.

"I knew you were going to say yes," he said, turning around and pointing with his finger at the showerhead above my head. I looked extremely uncomfortable as I realized that I had also finished taking my shower, turning off the showerhead as quickly as I could.

When it was off and I couldn't feel the water running down my body anymore and everything was silent around me, I felt even more uncomfortable than before. I had my back turned to my mate and I felt as if he was watching me, even though that couldn't be the case.

The man was one of the straightest men I knew in my life and I knew that he was probably thinking about his girlfriend right now.

I was pretty sure they were going to meet up soon, too. I heard that she went traveling to another country and wasn't going to be back until a couple of months from now.

I pushed that thought out of my mind, finished drying my body with a towel before turning around and noticing that Edward was looking at me.

He was just looking at me, which was weird and a little arousing at the same time. I didn't know if his cock was naturally that big when he wasn't aroused, but it caught my attention and I couldn't turn it away.

He was cut just like I was and wasn't ashamed of it. Why should he be? I asked myself. Pretty much everyone in the country was.

I couldn't help but think that he was much bigger than me, even though we never measured our dicks. Someone with his level of self-esteem would be laughing about the way I was thinking about us, which was one reason why I was pretty sure he would never even propose something like that.

But then something flashed across his eyes and I knew he was thinking about it.

I was sure of that, so much so I wasn't surprised when he said, "Andrew, come closer."

"What?" I asked, wondering what else was going on in his

mind.

"I asked you to come closer. I know the kind of person you are. You're always very submissive."

"No, I'm not. You got it wrong. I'm never submissive to any-one."

He chuckled, glancing down and looking at my cock.

"I don't want to boast about it, but I think I'm much bigger than you."

I glanced down, knowing where that came from, but wishing I didn't. It was one thing having thoughts that shouldn't be in my mind, and another to have my mate suggest that he was bigger than me. What was going on in his head?

He was playing with my sense of pride in myself and it wasn't going to work. Even though I was curious about it – I wanted to think about it when I was jacking off in my bathroom at night – I wasn't going to do anything so gay. I was so sure of that that I stood my ground.

"Come on. Come closer. I promise I won't bite," he said, raising his voice as his eyes started to look more frightening. I didn't know what was about Edward, but he always had such a presence that he always made me do whatever he wanted.

I didn't want to admit it, but the control he had over me was making me do it. I took a step forward and then another and one more before I found myself shuffling toward him, incapable of stopping myself. In no time at all, I was then right by his side.

He moved so that we were even closer and I could feel the heat of his body pulsing to me. I noticed that he was slightly taller than me again and I watched with utmost attention as he put his fingers around his cock.

I didn't know if it was his hand that was big, but he barely managed to touch his thumb to his fingers, which was surprising. His cock just looked so much thicker than mine I was surprised he could do that.

"Man, what are we even doing?" I asked, flashing a smile as I hoped he was going to say that he was just pulling my leg.

But the serious look on his face was telling me another story. He wanted this to go on and it looked like he planned on it happening a long time ago. I didn't want to think he was bicurious, but the possibility was up in the air.

"We are measuring how big we are. I've always wondered about that."

My body froze up. It was like Edward was reading my mind all the time, which was impossible. Either that or whatever he could see on my face was telling him everything he needed to know.

"You know how gay this is."

"It's not gay as long as we aren't touching each other and, even though we are very close to doing that, I know I won't."

He started to stroke his cock, making it look even bigger and thicker than normal. In a matter of seconds, he was fully hard and raging. It was only that way because Edward *was* turned on. Either he was very curious about it or he had a very volatile ego. I didn't think the latter was the case, but it was as if it was.

"Aren't you going to do anything?" He said, suggesting that I should make my cock hard as well.

My hand was frozen. I knew I shouldn't move it, but I had no other choice. Outside, I couldn't hear anything, even though the soccer field was by the side of the building and I knew that our training was still going on. It wasn't finished yet. When it was, the other players would be storming into the bathroom and would catch us in the act.

"Fine," I said through gritted teeth, looping my fingers around my dick and hoping that this was going to end soon. Even though I was aroused and it was the first time we were bonding this way, I never thought it would happen. Not only that, but I was also sweating coldly. It was the first time I was sweating so much, even after a cold shower.

"That's more like it, man," Ed said jokingly, still moving his hand up and down along his stick. It was big, his hand taking seconds to cover the whole distance from the cockhead to the base of the shaft.

One other reason why I didn't want to be doing this was that I knew I wasn't as big. But since he was willing to go through everything to prove that to me once and for all, I couldn't do anything to stop him.

I was still stimulating my dick when Ed said, "Stop. That's good enough."

And just like the submissive idiot I was, I obeyed him yet again. When I took my hand off my dick, he did the same as he analyzed our shafts. A second later, a smile started to appear on his face as he realized that the answer he was looking for was the truth.

"Damn, man. You're so tiny it's almost laughable."

My body was shaking as I said, "Can we just stop this now? It's making me feel so weird and awkward."

He glanced at the door to the bathroom, answering, "I don't think so. There's still one more thing I want to do."

CHAPTER 3

I still had no idea what was going on in his head, but Edward was satisfied with the results. So much so that I thought he was going to put his clothes back on and was going to walk out of the building. Moments later, though, when I realized that wasn't the case, he flashed a smile as he made a circular movement with his finger.

"Turn around."

"Why?" I asked, now feeling as if I was in some kind of dream and that nothing of this was happening. After all, before now, Edward never behaved this way. He was always pushy, knew that he could impose whatever he wanted on anyone, but right now it was as if he was trying to control everything I wanted to do.

And it was working. As much as it pained me to be saying so, it was working. I was doing everything Ed wanted.

Even though my belly was very cold, I turned around so that he could see my behind. I was conflicted about it. Even though it was making me feel turned on, to the point I was happy that my erection had another reason to be existing right now, I knew that this could lead to something we'd both regret. And if it led to that, the last thing I wanted was everyone on campus finding out that I was something else other than another straight dude.

"Satisfied now?" I hissed, hoping that was going to be enough and he was going to just walk out of the building with me. Then, I expected a very detailed explanation from him about this.

This whole thing was getting out of control and I couldn't make sense of it. What the hell was going on here?

"Not yet," he replied, just watching me and doing nothing else. Time was passing and my dick was so hard, my balls so tense I felt as if time was dilating.

It was the first time I was naked before another man and it was… I didn't know if I could put it into words, but I guessed it was kind of liberating, maybe? I was definitely enjoying it, even though I didn't want to admit that.

We were playing soccer not too long ago. That was all we were doing, and now my mate was checking out my behind. I had no idea what was going on in his mind, but it couldn't be anything trivial.

"Satisfied now?" I asked through gritted teeth, wishing I could punch his face, or even get down on my knees so that I was sucking him off. Jesus. I had no idea I could even think that way of Ed, and it was disconcerting. It was making it more difficult for me to say that I really wasn't interested in men.

"That's good enough," he said and I turned around slowly, even though I knew I shouldn't. His eyes were still going up and down slowly, checking me out.

Edward was being so weird, and he wasn't even drunk.

I noticed that his hand was still pumping his cock gently, and it was still hard and pointing at me. It was difficult for me not to look down at it. It was hard not to think and wonder what it would be like to suck him off, even though I knew that was gay and thus it was something that I could never do.

He flashed a smile, asking, "Tell me, Andrew, have you ever sucked another guy off?"

I took a step backward, finding it impossible to wrap my head around what he just asked. It was one thing being naked in front of him and another hearing what he just said.

"What?"

He shrugged, explaining, "If you've never done it before, you can't know for sure that you aren't gay."

"But I'm not!" I affirmed, stomping the floor. "This is ridiculous. Now you're going to tell me that I should suck you off just to prove that I'm not gay."

"Well, I wasn't going to suggest that, but now that you mentioned it, I suppose we should just get on with this as quickly as possible. After all, I don't want to waste time when there's no reason to do that."

"Hmmm… what?" I asked, not understanding anymore where any of this was going.

Either way, it was difficult not to do what he wanted, mostly because I couldn't shake off the feeling that I'd always been meant to be doing this. Not to mention that his stare and presence alone were too imposing, and I couldn't do anything about those things.

I couldn't help but sigh, getting on my knees and telling myself that I wasn't going on with it. I was going to stand up, get my clothes, throw them on, and walk out of here without saying anything else.

But then again… I was curious. He was so much bigger than me and part of me was wondering what it would be like to suck him off – or at least, to do something similar while nobody was looking. We were in the bathroom, it didn't seem that any of the other players were going to walk in soon, and I had all the time in the world…

Or perhaps not all the time in the world, but that was nothing more than a detail.

I was on my knees right before his shaft, and I couldn't stop staring at it. It was pointing right at me, and I noticed that I didn't have to lower my head much to suck it off, if I was planning on doing that. It was difficult to make a decision on that without feeling as though I was betraying something fundamental about my being.

He was stroking his shaft gently, smiling, "You're not going to do it after all? You know that I can't force you to do anything, but

I'm kinda feeling disappointed right now..."

Fuck.

It was difficult not to do what he wanted when he was being so demanding. I was telling myself that I was only doing this because he was so imposing, but deep in my mind, I knew that it meant something else.

I shook that thought out of my mind and focused on something else.

The aroma that was coming from his junk was nothing short of very enticing. It was impregnating my lungs and I didn't know what to do about it. My eyes dissected his balls, making me want to touch them, but I didn't think I could play with them right now. I couldn't anger him.

He looked ahead at the door, saying through gritted teeth, "Just get on with it already. You're making me waste my time, and you don't know how angry I can get when someone doesn't respect my time."

There was no point not doing what he wanted, so I lowered my head as time appeared to be dilating before my eyes. When my lips touched his cockhead, it was like fireworks were exploding in my mind. I never felt so much pleasure in my life, wondering if I would feel the same if I licked the cunt of a woman.

I didn't think it would happen anytime soon, I thought in sorrow. I didn't have enough courage to approach a girl, even though I knew my body was begging me to do that.

"There, there. That's a lot better," he hissed, making me feel happy that he was approving what I was doing. I was the kind of guy that was always very competitive, and I wanted to show my mate that I was doing it right, even though by 'it' I was mentioning that I was giving him a blowjob.

I finished wrapping my lips around his shaft, applying pressure with it as if it was my duty to show him I could give him an excellent blowjob.

I didn't even know why the thought was even in my mind, but

it was there and I couldn't push it out.

"Excellent. You're better at this than I thought," he murmured, putting his hand on my head and starting to dictate what I should be doing. Goddammit, that was really happening and I couldn't do anything to stop it.

Ed had such a hold on me that I was pretty sure no one else felt the same way regarding him. Not even his girlfriend, who was just a slut. I never said that to his face, even though I'd always wanted to.

He groaned, pulling out when I thought he was going to come in my mouth. And the most striking thing about that? It was that I wasn't holding anything back. I was sucking him off, moving my head up and down along his shaft, and I was enjoying it all...

"We should do more of this," he said, finally turning around and putting his clothes on without saying anything else. I was left stupefied when he left the room, leaving me all alone.

I didn't know what was going to happen now, but there were a lot of nagging thoughts swirling in my mind at the moment, and I needed to deal with them.

CHAPTER 4

I was in his dining room with his mates. They were all chatting and joking happily with themselves, ignoring me. I knew that I wasn't anyone important, but I thought I was at least something to them. I cut off a piece of the steak on my plate, put it into my mouth, and started to chew it.

Edward was by my side, chatting with his friends happily. He couldn't stop smiling. He also couldn't stop stealing glances at me, as if he knew that what we did in the college's bathroom would never change. It could never be erased.

I was still chewing the piece of the steak when, moments later, I felt his hand on my thigh. I snapped my head in his direction, wondering what he was thinking that he was doing right now.

Our eyes met and I thought he was going to say something, but he didn't. He just kept staring at me, moments later moving his hand up over my thigh.

I thought he was going to touch my junk, but he didn't. I knew what I should be doing right now. I should be angry at him for taking advantage of me, but it was difficult to do that when we were among his mates.

I was his mate, too, but I felt that we were becoming more than that. Not to mention that I was soon going to have two confront him about what we did in the bathroom. After all, I couldn't stop thinking about it.

It was the day after yesterday, when we did that, and I was so obsessed about it that I didn't even sleep that night.

I couldn't even savor the steak I was eating. It was like it didn't mean anything as long as I couldn't figure out what was going on in my mind.

"What the hell are you doing?" I hissed, wondering if he was going to answer.

But then he flashed a smile as everything around me went silent. It wasn't that everyone noticed what was going on, but that my mind tuned out their chatter and laughter.

The only thing that mattered right now was the man seated by my side. He had me under his control again and I was powerless to stop him. Not to mention that his hand on my thigh felt really good. I had a pretty short pair of shorts, which allowed his hand to be in direct contact with my skin.

"You can't hide it. I've always been very confident about my sexuality, but with you, things are very different. You want me to be doing this with you, don't you?" He asked, doing so in such a way it was as though he was probing me for the right answer.

"I only did it to prove to you that I didn't like it at all," I responded, even though my dick was hard and it was getting harder as time passed. I was beating myself up that I was letting this happen. If I stood up right now, everyone would notice my boner, which was something I could never let happen.

After all, they still thought I was the kind of guy that would never do what I did the day before.

"And did it work?" He asked, moving his hand further up. My heart was beating so fast and I was sweating coldly. I almost thought I was going to have a heart attack.

I bit my bottom lip. It was difficult to go up against Edward. He always said the right thing at the right time, and it was happening now, too. He had me cornered up against myself. The moment I gave him that blowjob, he had me wrapped around his finger – more so than before.

He was playing me like I was his doll and I felt powerless

against him. So much so I was beginning to wonder if that was my destiny all along.

"I knew you weren't going to say anything," he murmured, now touching my junk with his hand. His fingers were grazing against my balls and even though I didn't want to admit this, it was arousing me.

I was beginning to wonder if I shouldn't just have sex with him. I couldn't read his mind as he could mine, but I was very sure that the thought must have crossed his mind at least once since he allowed me to give him head.

I picked up the glass of juice that was on the table and took a long gulp of it, trying to wet my dry throat. It didn't work. It wasn't that my throat was actually dry. After all, I hadn't even spoken much yet. I was just doing my thing, trying to look like I was the least important person in the room.

"You are such a jerk I'm wondering if I should keep being your friend."

"Well, you know you can do whatever you want, but it won't change who you are. You are mine. I can do whatever I want with you because I know you'll always agree to it."

I bit my bottom lip, Edward moving his hand so that it was cupping my junk. Applying pressure with his fingers, he was arousing me so much it was making it very difficult for me not to moan right now. I couldn't let anyone else at the table figure out that we were doing this.

All the masks were down. I wasn't going to say that I was interested in men, but I was into Edward, and he knew that.

So much so that he was getting more confident that nobody was going to notice anything. He even shifted his chair so that he was even closer to me, his fingers playing with my junk.

I tried cutting off another piece of the steak that was on my plate, but I didn't have the strength to put it into my mouth.

Sweat was pooling on my forehead and I felt like the room was over 120°. I felt like I was in a sauna room.

"Stop this. Someone is going to notice it and then… I don't know what we would have to say, but it would be so difficult we wouldn't be able to come up with anything convincing."

"Why should I stop it when I know you are enjoying every moment of this?" He asked, doing what I thought was beyond his capabilities. I didn't think he was so daring.

Edward snuck his fingers under my shorts, looping two of them around my cockhead. He started to stroke it gently, applying just enough pressure with them to make me want more. I parted my lips, locking my eyes with his as I wondered if he was going to kiss me, on top of everything he was already doing.

"But someone's going to notice this!" I hissed.

He tsked, saying, "Don't worry about it. I'm going to make sure nobody does. After all, this isn't the first time I'm doing this with another guy."

I shouldn't be surprised by what he said, but I still was. I widened my eyes at the same moment, Edward growing so much more confident that he put the entirety of his hand under my shorts and looped all of his fingers around my shaft.

I wasn't just hard right now. I was raging. I was on the verge of coming and there was nothing I could do to stop it. Noticing what was going on, he moved his hand up, squeezing my cockhead slightly before he pulled his hand out.

Then, very slowly, he put his hand back on top of the table and shouted, "Hey, everyone, wanna hit the pool? I'm dying to go there. It's so hot in here."

I let out a sigh of relief, even though I knew that things were far from over between us. Edward stood up, rushed out with everyone to where the swimming pool was, and then I couldn't see him anymore. As the last guy went through the door and I was left all alone, I wondered what was going to happen next.

I didn't have to go to the swimming pool, but how could I pass up the chance to see my friend without his shirt *and* shorts?

The answer was that I couldn't and so I went there with him.

CHAPTER 5

I didn't know what I was doing, but Edward was on top of me, his lips almost as if he was going to kiss me. Everyone had left the party and we were alone by the house. It was dark outside, the moon rising above the buildings.

He was breathing slowly, still quite wet after swimming in the pool for as long as he did. I couldn't swim with him for as long. I didn't have the stamina or the courage to do that, and there was a very good reason behind that. I couldn't hide my erection when I was in the pool, and I was so turned on then that I thought I was going to come.

Thankfully, that didn't happen.

But something much more surprising was happening right now. I didn't know how it came to this, but he had me pinned down on the tiled ground around the swimming pool. His hair was falling from his head, his eyes locked with me.

His muscles still looked so perfect, even under the dim light coming from the moon behind the clouds. His shorts were soaked and I could see his boner. Edward was just as aroused. He would never say that to me, but I was pretty sure that he couldn't hide it.

"Caught you…" He murmured all of a sudden, making me ask what was going on in his mind right now. It didn't matter if we kissed. I knew that it would never happen, but I was pretty sure he was planning on doing something else with me.

"What?" I asked, doing everything in my power not to grope

his body. I could feel his warmth all around me, making me as wet with the pool's water as much as I was sweating. My heart was pounding in my chest, and I couldn't do anything about it. I was just so confused, worried, and nervous.

"Caught you looking that time when I was changing in the locker room and, since then, I couldn't stop thinking about you," he murmured, sticking his tongue out and licking my cheek. Wow. I didn't think he'd ever do that, and it was hot as balls. I wished he'd do that again, but I didn't think he would. Edward was more preoccupied with whatever else he wanted to tell me.

I remembered the moment in our lives he was talking about. There had been that one time when I noticed him changing for the first time when we were together in the locker room. Even before then I knew his body was perfect, but I was still surprised by what I saw.

"I wasn't looking. Not for the reason you're thinking I was."

"No, man, I know why you were looking, and now I'm confirming everything," he murmured, licking me again with his tongue. This time, he went down as he licked my neck too, his fingers undoing the buttons of my shirt. I was so stupid, coming here to their little party with a polo shirt. I looked so awkward among them. They were so casual at the party.

"You smell really nice, and you also taste perfect," he said, taking in what his eyes were seeing. After he finished removing the last button of my shirt, he widened his eyes as he looked mesmerized by what he was seeing.

He was admiring my naked chest, which was something I never thought he would do. After all, there was nothing impressive about it. It was lean, a little defined, but nothing out of the ordinary. My chest wasn't shaped like a diamond like his was, which was one of the reasons why I wanted to be touching his body right now.

His muscles looked very tense. They were so tense that they were looking even more defined than they usually were.

I wanted to touch them, but not without Ed's permission.

He lowered his head, playing with my nipple as his hand started to massage my junk through my shorts. I looked around me to make sure that nobody was coming. I couldn't hear footsteps coming in this direction, which was enough to calm me down, but it wasn't enough to make me feel comfortable about this.

I put my hands against his chest and tried to move him away, but it was impossible. He was still pinning me down against the ground, massaging my junk more quickly and strongly as he hit all the sweet spots. I could only moan and groan, wishing I could take this to my bedroom so that we had all the privacy we needed.

He pulled his head back with a plop and I noticed that my nipple was very wet. The smile that appeared on his face didn't lie about what he was thinking right now. He enjoyed sucking on my nipple and I knew he was planning on doing the same to my other nipple.

When he moved his head there, I put my hand against his face as I tried to stop him. But I wasn't doing that because I wasn't enjoying this, but because what he just did left me breathless. I couldn't even control what my mind should be thinking.

"What's going on?" He asked, moving his finger around my other nipple. He was teasing me and it was working.

"I need to breathe. It's too much."

"I think that was enough time for breathing already," he grumbled, diving his head onto my other nipple before latching his lips around it. He applied enough pressure with it to make me feel that I was going to black out. His hand still playing with my balls and cock, I could only wonder what else he had planned for us.

Could it be that Edward was considering breaching me with his shaft? I didn't know, but the thought of being violated that way was nothing short of alluring. My mind was almost begging me to let him do that.

When he was satisfied with what he was doing, he pulled his

head back and locked his eyes with me again. But his hand was still against my crotch and I knew that meant we were far from done.

"I want to give you a little gift," he murmured, sneaking his fingers under my shorts and lowering them.

I didn't have enough time to react and I wouldn't have done anything to stop Edward anyway. My dick was free seconds later, pointing at him. I had about half a second to wonder what he meant by 'gift' before it was too late and he was already putting his lips around my dickhead, sucking on it.

The moment he was doing that, it was like he opened Pandora's box. Everything that I was containing inside me came out, telling everything I needed to know. I was into men. There was no denying that I was. I wasn't going to end my experience with just Edward, too.

"Holy shit. This is so good," I murmured, closing my eyes and focusing my attention entirely on us.

He lifted his head and said, "Really? I knew you were going to say that, which is why I'm so happy that you're feeling this way. I guess you should know that we aren't stopping here."

I knew we weren't, but hearing it from his mouth was intoxicating. When his lips weren't on my cockhead anymore, I felt like I was going back to being my usual self, always hammering into my mind that I could never do this. I felt like I was lying to myself.

Even though I was also into women, there was no denying that men could also do the same things, and they could be just as good.

He was working my shaft so well that I couldn't contain it when it happened. My dick started to throb and shake violently, milk coming out in hot, long spurts. And the best thing about that? It was that he decided to swallow everything, which was more than I thought he could ever do for me. After all, Edward had always been just about himself and no one else.

When he pulled his head back again, he smiled as I noticed my sperm smearing his lips. It was covering them partially. I didn't feel disgusted by that. I actually felt even more turned on now that

I was seeing that.

Then, he lazily stood up before he went to the door into the house. He turned his head to look at me before saying, "I'm going to prepare everything for something I know you want badly. It will be amazing."

I held out my hand as if I was going to grab him, but then he just jumped into the house and disappeared. I heard his footsteps running up to the second floor of the house and I knew that this was my cue to get out.

I didn't go after him, but I went to the bathroom and changed my clothes.

I needed to go back home and reflect on everything that happened.

CHAPTER 6

Edward was standing in front of me, holding something in his hand. I didn't need to read the label to know what it was. A bottle of lube. It was just like I thought this was going to be. The room was dark and we were doing this at night.

We were in my apartment. Edward said that we could only be doing this here, and I concurred with him. There was something different I couldn't put my finger on about having my first time with another man in my room.

He looked up, finding my eyes.

"You are a virgin, right?" He asked, prodding one of my deepest wounds. I was over 20 already and I hadn't had sex with a woman yet, which was very disconcerting. I was with someone else that was much more experienced. He knew what he was doing, how to press the right buttons to make me do anything he wanted, and it was working.

Just like in all the other times we were alone, he was getting everything his way.

He put the bottle of lube back down on the nightstand, climbing up on me as he laid me down on the bed. His hands worked fast to take off my shirt and I didn't do anything to stop him. Then, he lowered my shorts and took them off, too.

His fingers ripped off my pair of briefs and I heard the material being torn.

It happened so fast I didn't even register it properly. One moment I was fully dressed in my clothes and the next I was naked, the crush I had always been obsessed over right on top of me. It was so reminiscent of the time we were by the swimming pool at his friend's house.

"I know how much you want this," he murmured, looping his fingers around my shaft and pumping it. As he did that, I closed my eyes and focused my attention entirely on the way he was moving his hand up and down.

"I'll do anything for you." And I knew that, by saying that, I was sealing my life with his and that nothing would ever change that.

Moments later, he stopped jacking me off and proceeded to turn me around on the bed. I was put with my knees against the mattress, my butt pointing up.

His hands roamed around it, making me wonder when his fingers were going to be nudging my orifice. I was just waiting for that to happen, and I knew that it couldn't be stopped. The swirl of different feelings in my mind was nothing short of jaw-dropping.

I wasn't just going to lose my virginity right now. It was going to happen to another guy, and he was going to take my ass' virginity, too. Now that I was thinking about it, he never said that he wanted me to do anything else. He wanted to take my butt's v-card and nothing else.

My first time… I never thought that it would happen this way, but here it was, and it was everything I thought it was going to be.

His hands stopped moving and then he moved one of his fingers to my orifice. Nudging it, he drew moans out of my mouth I didn't think I could pull off. They were powerful, reverberating through the whole room. It was nigh impossible hearing anything through the walls, but what just happened was probably heard by my neighbors.

And the best thing about that? It was that I didn't care about it at all.

He pressed his finger against my orifice, making my whole

body shake. I knew what was going on in his mind. He was obsessed with me and wanted to be inside of me right away. And even though that was what was in his mind, he was going to take his time.

He was going to be rough when he was inside of me, but until then, he was going to be careful. He was going to ease me into what we were doing. I could see that in the way he was pressing his finger against my orifice, drawing circles over it.

When I thought he was getting tired, he moved so that his head was by the side of my head. I could feel his hot breath against my ear and I could do nothing against it. I was powerless to stop this dominating jock from doing anything and I wouldn't have it any other way.

The smile on his face was telling me everything. I couldn't see the entirety of it, but what I could see was enough to send shivers down my spine.

"I've been waiting for this for so long," he murmured into my ear. His body was so hot he was making the air around me warmer than it already was. I could feel his skin slightly grazing against mine and it was one of the best sensations in the world.

"I hope I won't disappoint you," I hissed and he widened his smile. I could tell what he was thinking right now.

More or less, I corrected myself. Edward was still so difficult to read sometimes – or most of the time, being honest about it.

"I'm sure you won't," he said, now pressing two of his fingers against my asshole. I moaned, urging him to put his fingers inside of me, even though I was pretty sure he was already planning on doing that as soon as possible.

The thing was that I was feeling very impatient right now. It was one thing thinking that I would never lose my virginity and another to be experiencing that, even though I knew it was going to take a little time until he was ready for it.

I could hear his hand going up and down along his massive cock. The taste of it I had before was mind-blowing and I wanted to savor it again as soon as possible.

I purred when I felt him moving down again, putting his head right where my ass was. I knew what he was planning on doing and I was overly excited about it already. Anyone looking at me now would be laughing at me for the way I was reacting.

"Are you ready for this, Andrew?" He asked, making me nod. But it appeared that he didn't notice that, because moments later he was already asking, "I'm going to touch my tongue to your asshole. Are you afraid of that?"

I felt more shivers running down my spine. It was one thing knowing that he would eventually do that, and another to be experiencing it.

I had shaved before and was ready for it. I took care of all the hair and cleaned up my rectum so that he didn't feel turned off when he was inside of me.

He was looking at my asshole right now and I could feel the vibrations of his excitement in the air. He knew that my asshole was very soft, hairless, and ready for his entry.

"I'm ready for everything you have for me," I said, hearing a slap echoing in the room when it happened. Then, he settled his hands on my ass, moving them around and around, almost like he was further preparing what he was going to do to me.

"That's the answer I wanted from you," he purred, putting his tongue out before touching it against my asshole. When he wiped it upward for the first time, I shut my eyes as I felt like stars were exploding in my field of vision.

He was still with his head right behind my ass before he said, "That was just one swipe of my tongue. There are so many more to come. I'm going to ask you again: are you ready for them?"

I just nodded. Speaking was impossible right now and he knew that. It was why he was happy with the answer he got, moving his tongue up and down against my orifice. He was wetting it so much I was wondering if he was even going to need the bottle of lube.

After one last swipe with his tongue, he pulled his head up as he looked satisfied. The dirty smile on his face didn't lie, after all. He wanted more and he was going to get more. After all, that was his style. Edward always got whatever he wanted.

"I like it that you cleaned yourself up before coming here," he murmured after moving so that his head was by the side of my head. Just like before, I could feel his hot breath against my face and it was one of the best things ever.

Similar to a previous moment, I didn't say anything. It was difficult controlling my breath and doing anything else. At this moment, I was just waiting for him to do the next best thing about our sex. He was going to penetrate me and breach all of my defenses, which I was sure was going to hurt a lot, but it was still what I wanted.

When he grabbed the bottle of lube, I knew that was what was going to happen now.

CHAPTER 7

"I've been waiting for this. It's so different when I take someone's virginity and even more so when it's a guy's," he commented and his voice was so weak I almost couldn't make it out. I was only able to do so because everything around us was quiet. We couldn't even hear a peep coming from the nearby roads.

He spread the lube around his cock, making me wonder if he was going to take his time with that. The reason I was thinking that way about it was that I was just so impatient I was already feeling anxious. I was aware that feeling anxiety was a constant in my life, but this was getting out of control.

It was the first time I was feeling so anxious I felt like I was going to explode.

He caressed my skin, moving his hand across my lower back.

What he was doing was enough to make me remember that he was the one in control, always, even though I didn't need that reminder per se. I was only thinking that because it made me feel much more alive and submissive than I already was.

He spread some lube on his hand, grabbing my waist with his hands before pulling me to him, pressing his cockhead against my waiting orifice. I was gripping the bedsheets so tightly I didn't think it was possible to grip them more strongly than I already was. Not only that, but our combined sweat was soaking them, too.

He breached the first barrier, then the next, going all the way in until he was pushing against my prostate. I bit against my bottom lip more tightly than I already was, drawing out blood. The pain that was searing my body was like anything I had ever felt.

And Edward wasn't even doing anything special. He just stood there, with his cock inside of me, and I was waiting to find out if he was going to start to ram it against me. But time was passing and nothing was happening.

I just cracked open my eyes when he started to roll his hips, almost as if he was reading my mind. I thought before that the pain I was feeling was already overwhelming, but now it was much more than that.

And the best thing about that? It was that he didn't even increase his pace beyond the one he was using. Ed was very slow and methodical, performing long strokes with his hips.

I could feel the entirety of his body against mine, knowing that it was going to be difficult to be without him inside of me when he pulled out.

Then, Edward murmured into my ear, "Gosh, you're so tight."

I couldn't say thanks. It was already impossible to say anything before and now it was even more so.

"I'm going to kick things up a notch. Are you ready for that?"

Just like minutes ago, I could only grit my teeth before he started doing that. He started to pound against my ass, his balls slapping my butt cheeks. It was incredible. My body was as though it was resonating with his, and we were moving with the same rhythm.

"So, so tight…" He murmured into my ear, his rod throbbing inside my rectum as he came without a condom on. I didn't worry about it, just letting the pleasure I was feeling from this wash over my body.

"And just as I knew from the beginning, you are now my bitch," he said again and I knew that his affirmation meant a lot more than what I thought it meant. I knew that it was riddled with other plans he had in store for me.

"I want to be your bitch for the rest of my life," I said even though I knew it meant that I was giving myself up for him for as long as he wanted, which could very well end up being the rest of my life.

His dick gave one last spasm inside of my rectum and then he pulled out, plopping down onto the bed. I followed suit, falling onto the bed. Then, I started to feel something I never thought I would. I wanted him to put his arms around me, but he didn't. He was just on the other side of the bed, not moving.

I peered over my shoulder before I realized he was already sleeping. It seemed that our sex took quite a toll on him, which was nothing short of what could be expected.

Still, I couldn't help but wait impatiently for the part, where I said I was going to be his bitch, could entail.

I knew I was going to be his sex servant for the rest of my life, but then what else?

The End

Looking for the first three books of the series? Find them below. The next page has a steamy sneak peek, too. Go check it out!

1. Caught Looking by the Quarterback

2. Caught Looking by the Basketeer

3. Caught Looking by the Dropout

Lastly, leave a review if you liked the book. It always helps me so much!

SNEAK PEEK: CAUGHT LOOKING BY THE QUARTERBACK

Straight to Gay First Time Story (Bicurious Guys - 1)

I was just a college guy, like all the others. I was trying to fit in and look less like an idiot. Why did I have to stumble into the college's football team, though? I didn't know, but things were working out this way. More and more girls were beginning to show interest in me, even if it was only momentary… and I didn't think it was going to lead anywhere.

I sighed, closing the door by my side when I realized someone was there. Not too far from me, taking off his shirt and getting ready to put on his uniform. I supposed it was appreciation more than anything that was making me feel this way about the guy, even though I was 100% straight. Really, I was, and nothing was going to change that.

But nothing could have gotten me ready for what I was seeing. The guy was perfect. He was in his early twenties, so he was a little older than me, huge, with rippling muscles, and a beard still to be made. His hair was jet-black and his eyes the color of emerald. Every time he looked at me, he froze me with his gaze.

I couldn't stop thinking about him, even when he was in his room and wasn't doing anything more than playing on his computer. I wasn't going to say I was gay. I really wasn't, but I couldn't stop admiring him for being everything I wanted to become. Perhaps he could help me with working out at the gym, but then I didn't know if I'd be able to hide my boner… like it was happening now.

Not only I wasn't gay, but I also had to keep reminding myself that I wasn't a virgin, either. Not in the usual, more common sense of the word, at least. I had some experiences where it kind of happened with some girls… And I'd like to keep things at that.

Austin was now taking off his pants too, and I couldn't stop dissecting his perfect legs with my eyes. I couldn't help but imagine what it would be like to slide my hands over his muscles, feeling his hair, the curves that defined his legs, and smelling the scent of his crotch. Why was I thinking about those things of my team's leader?

I didn't know, but I was already feeling desperate and my boner was beginning to show. I came here with a common pair of jeans and it should be enough to keep it hidden. Austin could never find out that I had a huge turn-on for him, or else there would be trouble. This was a small college in the middle of nowhere, in a region known for being pretty homophobic. I didn't want to take the risk and then be forced to transfer to another university. It wasn't going to happen.

I took a deep breath and looked away quickly when he turned slightly. I didn't know if he was looking at me or not. We were in the dresser room and everything was pretty quiet here. Everything was so silent I could almost hear a pin dropping. I was a couple of feet away from Austin and I was pretty sure he wasn't thinking anything odd was happening here. After all, he had no reason to believe I was gay.

I took a deep breath in, looked back where he was, and I realized he was back to putting on his uniform. But he was still taking off his socks this time. He wasn't looking as imperious as before because he was seated now, his back turned to me.

But it wasn't that seeing him that way was making him look any less lust-inducing than he was. Even now, my body was frozen and I hadn't made much progress in terms of putting on my uniform. I needed to do that when my cock wasn't so hard. I should be punching myself that I was feeling those things for the guy that was always so willing to help everyone out, but it was just... impossible to control my feelings.

I heard the door opening and I knew that meant that things here were going to get more complicated. I could hear them talking out loud, cracking jokes, and laughing. It was the rest of the team. They were walking into the dressing room and were going to see that I was stealing glances at the quarterback...

BICURIOUS SERIES
AND MORE

GAY FOR BLUE COLLARS

1. Given to the Cop

2. Given to the Miner

3. Given to the Plumber

4. Given to the Firefighter

5. Given to the Mechanic

DIRTY FANTASIES

1. Filling in for the Bride

2. Filling in for the Wife

3. Filling in for the Girlfriend

ABOUT THE AUTHOR

Michael Levi's biggest passion? Writing steamy, romantic stories that leave his readers panting. He's currently focusing on Omegaverse and bicurious stories, but his collection is diverse and there are books for everyone's tastes. If you're looking for straight to gay, first time, BBC, ABDL, and more, you're going to find them on his author page.

He lives to pamper his readers, every kiss means a lot more than what meets the eye, and he loves his Alpha males. Making sure that every gay first time feels different, Michael Levi writes his stories with a cup of coffee by his side. And for inspiration, he always opens a photo of his new crush.